For Alison

~ **M.W.**

For the Millars
~ **P.H.**

Text copyright © 1995 by Martin Waddell
Illustrations copyright © 1995 by Paul Howard

First U.S. edition 1995

Waddell, Martin.
John Joe and the big hen / Martin Waddell : illustrated by Paul Howard.— 1st U.S. ed.
Summary: Abandoned by his older brother and sister and frightened by a big hen poking
around the barnyard, John Joe hides in a field and must be rescued by the dog.
ISBN 1-56402-636-1
[1. Farm life—Fiction. 2. Chickens—Fiction.]   I. Howard, Paul, 1967– ill.   II. Title.
PZ7.W1137Jo 1995   95-6306

10 9 8 7 6 5 4 3 2 1

Printed in Belgium

This book was typeset in Granjon.

The pictures were done in watercolor.

Candlewick Press
2067 Massachusetts Avenue
Cambridge, Massachusetts 02140

John Joe
— and the —
Big Hen

Martin Waddell
illustrated by
Paul Howard

CANDLEWICK PRESS
CAMBRIDGE, MASSACHUSETTS

"It's your day to look after John Joe," Mammy told Sammy, so he had to stay with John Joe. Mary read her book and Mammy went on with her work. Splinter the dog sat in the sun and toasted.

Sammy got bored looking after
John Joe. Sammy wanted to play
with his friend, Willie Brennan.
"I'm going down Cow Lane to the
Brennans'," Sammy told Mary.

"Take John Joe with you," said Mary,
but Sammy took Splinter instead
of John Joe.

"I'm all by myself!" John Joe told Mary.
"You'd better tell Mammy!"
"Let Mammy get on with her work,"
Mary said. "I'll deal with our Sammy!"
Mary took John Joe by the hand and
set off down Cow Lane to find Sammy.

They went to the Brennans', but there was no sign of Sammy! Mary was mad, for it wasn't her day to look after John Joe.

"Do you think they'd be down by the stream?" asked John Joe.

"I'd look, but you are too little to go," Mary said. "And I can't leave you here with no one to look after you."

"I'll look after myself!" said John Joe.

The Brennans' big hen came to
look at John Joe. John Joe was used
to the hens at his house, but he didn't
know the Brennans' big hen.
"I'm not scared of you!"
John Joe told the hen.
"I'll whack your backside,"
John Joe told the hen.

"Go away home, hen!"
John Joe told the hen . . .
but the big hen didn't go.

John Joe climbed on the wall,
for he thought that the Brennans'
big hen might eat him.

"MRS. BRENNAN!" shouted John Joe,
but Mrs. Brennan was out.

"MARY!" yelled John Joe, but Mary had gone after Sammy and she couldn't hear him.

"OH, MAMMY!" wailed John Joe, but Mammy was safe back at home.

That left John Joe alone with the Brennans' big hen and so . . . John Joe ran away from the hen!

Mary came back to the Brennans'
with Sammy and Splinter, but . . .

"Where's our John Joe?"
Sammy said.

"JOHN JOE!
JOHN JOE!
OUR JOHN JOE!"
shouted Sammy.

"JOHN JOE!"
shouted Mary.

No John Joe with the hens in the yard.

No John Joe with the pigs in the sty.

No John Joe in the ditch.

No John Joe in the barn.

"Go find John Joe, Splinter!" said Sammy.

Splinter walked around and sniffed
at the ground . . . and the wall . . .
and the top of the wall.
Then Splinter dove into the field.
Splinter barked and he barked
and he barked . . .

WOOF! WOOF! WOOF!

John Joe was
asleep in the field.

"The big hen chased me!" said John Joe.
"We thought you were lost," said Mary,
as she carried John Joe up the lane.

"John Joe was scared by the Brennans' big hen," Mary told Mammy. "He hid away in the field. We thought that we'd lost our little John Joe."
"There's no way I'm losing my little John Joe!" Mammy said.

"You were supposed to look after John Joe," Mary told Sammy. "Well, I looked after myself!" said John Joe.